The Well

Duane E. Coffill

The Well

Copyright © Duane E. Coffill, 2019

Dedication

For my parents, George and Marie Coffill. Dad, I miss our fishing days together. You will always be my role model and my hero. On March 9th, 2014, you left this Earth and went to Heaven. I miss you every day, and I love you. Mom, you are my number one fan and reader. Thank you for all your support in my writing. I love you, and I'm glad you're doing well enough to see your grandchildren, Madelyn and Savannah.

Norman Reeds and his golden retriever, Denny, were in the field playing. Norman was throwing a stick, and Denny would run and retrieve it. Norman was eleven years old while Denny was seven, and Norman's parents had just bought a house in Tucker Falls.

It was four acres, and Norman's parents got the house and the land for a reasonable price.

The land was half field and half lawn, which meant that part of the property had been upon while the other portion was not. The field had some overgrowth, but you were able to walk through it without the top of weeds irritating your arms. Norman had dark brown hair and hazel eyes. Denny was a golden retriever, and as they were playing, Norman noticed that they were getting further and further away from the house, and then, he saw it.

Denny was by his side while holding an old stick in his mouth that Norman had thrown for him. They were walking up to an old well. Norman saw Denny drop the stick by Norman's feet and he went over to the well, but Norman held him by his collar, and Norman looked at the well with its cement cap and the chipped sides with some weeds growing through the holes from years of abuse from the elements. There was a green fungus wrapped around the well on the bottom section.

A beautiful little stream was in front of it, and Denny walked over to it while licking the water and Norman knelt next to him. He reached into the water, and it was cold! He put his right hand into the stream and then scooped up the water in the palm of his hand, and he put it into his mouth and drank the fresh, cold liquid. He got up while keeping his eyes glued to the old well. Denny was close by as he followed Norman, and he felt the tall grass brush against his legs.

"What do you think, boy?" As Denny was wagging his tail and pressed against Norman's body, they both were looking at the well. The grass was tall all around, but near the well...it was suppressed, withered... dead.

Norman walked up to the well, and he gently placed his hand on the cement cover, and he touched it and felt the tiny holes and the roughness. Denny was sniffing around the well, and he walked around with his nose wriggling and tail wagging. Norman thought he heard something from within the well but wasn't sure.

Denny barked, and his barking got louder and louder as he started whimpering and he went over to Norman, pushing him away from the well. "What is it, boy? What's going on...?" Norman pushed away from the frantically barking Denny and kept looking back at the well. Then suddenly, Norman fell backward into the tall grass. He had tripped on an old cement block he didn't see earlier, and suddenly the well's cover moved.

Denny ran back to the well and continued his barking as Norman sat up and saw the well's cover moving slowly to the side and then, just as suddenly as it had started, it stopped. The cover had slid halfway, revealing a shrouded entrance, and Norman slowly got up. His jaw dropped, and he heard something, but couldn't make out the sound.

Denny kept barking at the well, and then...something grabbed Denny, sucking him into the darkness. Norman couldn't see what it was, but it was dragging Denny into the well and Norman ran up. He grabbed Denny's lower body and the poor beast was barking, then whimpering, but Norman lost his grip, and he realized that the lower part of Denny had fallen outside the well while his upper torso had been ripped off and pulled into the well. The lid slowly closed as Norman continued screaming.

"DENNY! DENNY…NO!!!" The cover had closed, and all that remained was Denny's lower body. Blood covered the ground and splattered over the well as it made its way to the stream. Portions of Denny's insides were on the ground, along with feces and other bodily fluids. Norm was crying uncontrollably. Denny's half-body quivered, and it startled Norman as he saw his friend being chopped in half as something took the other half into the well. Norman gripped Denny tightly, and from inside the well the sounds came a little muffled, but he knew…his best friend was gone.

Norman's tears were heavy as he looked at Denny's lower body in disbelief.

"DENNY…I'M SO SORRY I COULDN'T SAVE YOU..I'M SO SORRY…"

Norman slowly got up, with grass stains and mud on his pants and tears running down his cheeks.

He slowly got up while his legs were like rubber from the shock of what he just experienced and he ran to the house to get his parents while he quickly glanced back, hoping that whatever came out of the well was not coming after him. He ran through the tall grass, and he kept replaying the burning image of Denny crying and shrieking.

"MOM, DAD...MOM, DAD...HE'S DEAD! HE'S DEAD!" He saw his parents outside, as they were standing by the back of the house and peering at Norman. They had heard the screams, and they ran out to him as they met halfway but didn't know what was going on.

"MOM, DAD...DENNY'S DEAD! DENNY'S DEAD!" He was yelling and crying as his father embraced him, and his mother looked at his clothes, shocked at seeing blood.

"What happened?" she asked while kneeling next to him and embracing him, while his father looked down at him and asked what had happened.

"Norman?" his father asked, seeing the fear and the tears.

"Something took Denny...It TOOK him!" Norman said, still crying.

"OK, calm down. What happened?" His father asked again, seeing his son's eyes fill with tears, and his skin covered in blood.

"Norman, honey...what happened?" his mother reiterated, and she took him from her husband's arms, and she held him; she felt him shaking, and the blood on his clothes was still fresh as it smeared onto her hands.

He cried in his mother's arms as his father grabbed the shovel that had stood against the house and said, "I'll head out and check it out." He walked towards the field. Norman turned and told his father to be careful.

His father reassured him, "I'll be OK, Norman. Go inside the house with your mother." Ted turned towards the field once more and walked forward, closer to the evil in the well.

He walked into the tall grass, with his fingertips touching the tops of weeds with seeds on them, waiting to grow into pretty flowers that would cover the field with endless beauty.

Ted was almost at the scene where Denny had been killed, and then he saw the blood that had painted a part of the grass that was the closest to the well.

What happened here? Ted thought with horror as he checked out the scene, and some blood was still dripping into the brook like heavy drops of rain. He watched the stream carry the crimson pool down with it. He walked across the small brook and glanced at it, with his eyes glued to the top and he noticed there was something else besides the blood puddles.

He grew closer to his left as his foot was stepping in one of the puddles, and he noticed a print in the middle of the well, where the cover and the base met. It was as something had come out and grabbed Denny, and dragged him down into the well. There were traces of dog hair and blood smeared on the outside of the cover, indicating that Norman's story was true.

Ted couldn't believe what he saw. "Denny? Denny? Where are you, boy? Where you at?" Ted yelled, hoping to hear Denny barking or at the very least, responding somehow. He heard nothing, but the sweet sound of the running brook.

Whatever Norman saw, it must be true. All this blood must be from something. But did Norman see Denny get killed, and if so, by whom…or what?

Ted couldn't see what he saw, and then, he reached down and slowly pushed the cover off. It was heavy at first like it hadn't been open for years. As he pushed, he saw spiders and two snakes in the crevices of the well. The cracks and crevices were deep enough for anything small and silvery to slip in.

There was a green-slimy mucus coating the walls and a small vine climbing around the interior.

As Ted looked down into the well, he saw water, a pool of darkness, and blood running down the interior, indicating that Denny had been dragged down into the well. Oh my God…what Norman said might actually be true. Norman hasn't lied to me in the past, but telling us that something grabbed Denny from this spot was hard to believe, but now…I can almost believe him. Ted stared at the well, his eyes glaring at the blood as it ran down the interior of the well. He also saw scratches up and down the walls, and wondered if it had been Denny trying to escape or if the marks were from something else…

Ted closed the cover and ran back to the house to hide. The question that kept plaguing him was, according to Norman, the lower body of Denny had fallen onto the ground…but where did it go? What happened to Denny's remains? Ted thought, over and over. He didn't know what to think.

He closed the cover, with the clanging sound of the cement cover slamming roughly.

What could live in the water of a well? I've seen snakes and a few critters, but that's all. We live in Maine, and nothing can survive in a well...right? Ted walked back while speculating and with his knuckles slightly roughed up and covered in blood and dirt while walking through the tall grass. Norman was inside the house, sitting down on a kitchen chair and his mother gave him a washcloth, and she started to clean his forehead as Norman trembled.

"Norman, we need to talk, son," Ted said while sitting next across from Norman and he started to ask him some questions. "Norman, what happened out there?" Ted asked firmly while in disbelief, while not knowing what to believe. "Dad, I told you already, something took Denny, and it cut him in half...didn't you see the body?" His eyes filled with fear and as tears streamed down his cheeks.

"What I saw was nothing but blood and dirt, and I found no other half of Denny. His lower body was not there! I need to know what happened, Norman," Ted said firmly, feeling guilty at his son's terror, but he needed to know the truth.

"Dad, I know you don't believe me, but he WAS taken," Norman said, almost crying again. Ted went outside while Norman was being wiped down and Ted sat on one of the lawn chairs, looking into the field, feeling bad that Norman had lost his best friend.

I wish Dad would believe me...I wish whatever thing or monster would come out and show itself, but Dad probably still wouldn't believe me. I miss you, Denny... Norman thought, his eyes filling with tears once again. Norman lay in bed with his eyes wide open, and the image of Denny being pulled apart and his insides spilling over all over the ground and into the brook played on a disturbing loop in his mind. Norman felt guilty that he couldn't save his friend and Norman heard the faint cries of Denny as Norman thought about what he saw. It was haunting.

Ted was asleep in the chair while his wife was in bed with a mystery novel in hand. I miss you, Denny....I'm so sorry....I love you! She thought, and then, she fell asleep shortly.

Norman cried, and Ted ran into Norman's room as he sat on the bed and comforted him.

"Dad? I MISS DENNY! I MISS HIM A LOT!" Norman cried while Ted held him and started to tear up himself. He started to believe Norman, not because he had to think about it, but his heart was telling him that his son was honest. Ted held Norman while thinking on how he was going to deal with this fresh hell and if it was true...what kind of creature lived in that old well? Ted thought, not knowing what he was willing to do, but he knew he had to find out more about the well and how long it had been there since their family had moved in only seven months ago.

Norman recalled images of Denny running into his bedroom and jumping onto the bed, almost crushing Norman's nuts, but he missed his furry best friend, and the image of his hairy friend being cut in half was beyond painful and traumatizing.

***

Norman was asleep while Ted walked out and kept the bedroom door open and decided to go to bed. The next day, Norman was off with his mother, and Ted went into the field, and he noticed that the grass had been pushed down by something. He saw red beetles throughout the flattened grass. The crimson beetles looked like ladybugs, but without the spots. Their bodies were long like snails.

He picked up one of them and suddenly felt a sting and dropped it immediately. "SHIT!" The damn thing stung me!" After dropping it, Ted noticed that his finger was bleeding. He looked at the beetle and immediately stepped on it, crushing it as a green ooze emanated from the crushed insect.

The blood was still flowing from his fingertip, and Ted took his handkerchief from his back pocket and wrapped his finger around it until he got back inside the house. He continued his patrol of the area, and he kept checking the well's top, noticing that it had been moved. The cover was not completely on, as it was yesterday when Ted adjusted it.

A warm breeze came in and gently moved Ted's hair as he scanned the area, trying to find anything besides what he saw in the well. He decided to head back and take care of the bite or sting as the pain grew more severe. As he turned towards the house, he heard something. It was the sound of a cement cover sliding.

He turned quickly and stared at the well's cement cover but saw nothing! His eyes were peeled to the well as he waited for the sound to occur again, but only the wind and a few woodpeckers could be heard in the distance.

He turned his head towards the house and headed in. His boots stomped on the dried grass, and a slight concern grew within him. Night had fallen on the cold field as a chill came in, and it was a beautiful October Monday morning. A thin layer of frost coated everything as school was back in season, and Norman was waiting at the end of his driveway, but he kept looking towards the field, where the well hid its mystery.

The loss of Denny upon the family was like a thorn in the back of the neck you hoped would come out on its own, but the piercing of the thorn was more of a dull throbbing than sharp pain. Norman got onto the bus while remembering that Denny used to wait with him, and now that was a far distant memory, and Norman had no one.

"Hey Norman, where's Denny?" his friend Louis asked while Norman sat next to him, not wanting to answer. "Norman? Norman? Are you OK?" The boy's innocent voice was filled with curiosity and concern.

Norman turned to him while trying not to break down. "He's dead." His tone remained low as he watched Louis's face.

"I'm sorry. How did it happen?"

"He just...died, that's all. We'll talk about it later, OK?"

"Sure. I'm sorry to hear that. He was a good dog." Norman felt the compassion emanating from his friend, and deep down, he was angry and wanted to know what had come out of the well. Part of him was inclined to inform Louis of the truth, but he was also afraid. The trip to school was mentally exhausting, not from the schoolwork, but he felt that he was wasting his time and wanted to go to the well and see for himself if he might discover the truth.

Louis came home with Norman after school while his mother was cooking dinner and his father was still at work. Norman automatically looked towards the field where the mysterious well sat in its place, enduring the stream nearby and forever casting its spell of evil.

"Why do you keep looking into the field, Norman?" Louis asked with curiosity. Norman turned to Louis as they were walking on the porch. "I have to show you something, Louis." He put down his school stuff, and Louis followed suit.

As they were walking out to the well, their legs encountered the tall grass, and Norman grew worried. He wondered if it was a big mistake to bring his friend out to the well.

"Where are we going, Norman?"

"We're going out to the well."

"Why?"

"You'll see." Norman grew more anxious as they got closer and then alongside the brook running, and just over the small hump of grass, he saw the ugly cement hole in the ground with its rusted face staring down but seemed to crack a wicked smile as it saw the children approaching. "What is that, Norman?" Louis asked, his eyes still searching as the sun was slowly setting in their faces.

"This is what killed Denny. I don't know what's inside, but something dragged him inside and even cut him in half, but I don't know what did it."

"Holy shit, Norman! What's inside, do you think?"

"I wish I did, but I haven't opened the cover because I have no idea what it could be. I guess I'm afraid that whatever is inside might get me, too!" Norman wanted to open the cover now that he had his friend with him.

"Shit! Let's open it!" Louis said with intensity, as he wanted to know what was in the well besides stinky water and maybe some mice or garbage. Norman looked at him and walked to the well, and he was nervous but was trying to avoid showing it "Kids, dinner's ready...Come and wash up!" Norman's mother called from the porch as they heard and decided to get something to eat instead.

"Are we coming back out after dinner, Norman?" Louis asked, as he morbidly wanted to see the inside of the well for himself. Norman said, "After dinner, we will, but we might have to wait a little longer because I know my dad wouldn't want me out here." Louis peered at him. "What about tonight then? I can come over after my parents are asleep and I'll grab two flashlights, and then we can check it out."

Norman looked at him and nodded with great hesitation. Dinner was served, with everyone silent at the table and Norman and Louis were eating while Norman's parents were concentrated on something else.

***

Norman glanced at his father, who was using his fork and slowly moving his food around while his mother was staring at his fork and was immediately annoyed. Something was up!

Norman continued eating his food, and Louis was almost done, and he kept looking at the clock and waiting for his mother to pick him up.

The plan was for Louis to go home and then return later with flashlights, tools, and weapons for protection. The operation was less than organized, at the least. Norman gently put his fork down and took a sip of his Gatorade.

He wondered if Louis could make it tonight or not. He knew he didn't dare to do the operation alone, but he only hoped his friend would keep his word. There was a knock on the door, and Anna got up, and she went to the door and opened it. It was Louis's mom picking him up.

"He's been fed already, and you're welcome to have some dinner with us!" Anna chirped while guiding Louis's mother into the kitchen.

"No, thank you. I appreciate you feeding Louis."

Louis saw his mother, and he got up while grabbing his school bag that was leaning against his kitchen table chair. "OK, honey...thank them for dinner." Her voice was slightly high and seemed nice, but in a fake way.

"Thanks again for dinner. See you on Monday." Norman looked at him meaningfully and nodded while Ted smiled and Louis gave Ted a fist bump and then, Louis and his mother left.

"OK, honey. You need to take a shower, and whatever homework you have, I would suggest you finish it so that you have the entire weekend to play. Then maybe we can have Louis over for one night."

"That would be cool, but I can call tomorrow. Is that OK, Mom?" he asked.

"That's fine, sweetheart. Now go shower." Norman got up and headed into his bedroom. He grabbed underwear, socks, a T-shirt and some shorts. He always felt comfortable sleeping in shorts, especially in the fall.

"You're quiet today, hun. Are you all right?" she asked Ted while sitting back in the kitchen chair and taking a sip of her water. He looked at her and said, "I'm OK. I went out to the well yesterday, and there were these tracks around it, like a slug or something.

There were these green pebbles all over the ground, and I checked online at work, but I couldn't find anything."

His voice, filled with frustration, and Anna suggested, "A slug? What kind of animal could spit out green pebbles?" She looked over at Ted and saw he was distraught and determined to discover the truth.

Ted checked his computer again at home, but nothing! Norman was awake, and he slowly arose from bed with his heart beating fast, and he forgot that Louis would be on his way and that they were supposed to meet.

Shit! I forgot about how we would meet up...Maybe, he'll throw pebbles at my window like in the movies, but I can hear my Dad still up and probably checking on some stuff.

Norman slowly tip-toed into his bedroom and peered around the corner, where his father's PC was, and he peeked and saw his father was still working. He hoped that Louis wouldn't be stupid enough to knock on the door.

He watched his father slowly getting frustrated and hearing him say things like, "Son of a bitch! How come nothing is showing up...there is nothing about pebbles on the ground by wells, or anything!"

Suddenly, he watched his father get up from the computer chair, and he shut off the monitor and went to bed. Good, Dad's going to bed. Please, oh please, Louis doesn't be an idiot and knock on the door...! Norman slowly crept into the living room, and he heard his parents' bedroom closing, and then, it was shut.

He went back to his room and put on some regular clothes, especially since the well was the place they were headed tonight! He put on his old jeans from yesterday, and he made sure he grabbed a jacket, a flashlight, and something to use as a weapon.

Norman grabbed his aluminum bat, and he gripped it tightly, and he lightly stepped around the living room. He gently opened the door, and it squeaked a little, and he stopped while grinding his teeth in anticipation.

He tried again and then; it did the same thing. He opened the screen door and slowly went through and closed the door, and he walked quietly on the porch, especially as it was near his parents' bedroom.

He turned the flashlight on, and there was moonlight, which helped some with the light. He was pointing the flashlight all around, and he was looking for Louis. He decided to step down off the porch and onto the ground.

As he was moving his flashlight around, a yell ensued.

"NORMAN!" Norman jumped, but it was only Louis. "WHAT THE HELL, MAN?! YOU SCARED THE CRAP OUT OF ME!"

Norman tried not to yell, but Louis was grinning, and he said, "Gotcha!" He chuckled, and Norman punched his right shoulder.

"Ouch! What was that for?" Norman looked at him and said, "That was for scaring me, you asshole!"

"Sorry. Are we ready to do this?" Louis asked while carrying a black bag that contained a flashlight, a hammer, and a screwdriver.

"Wow! I guess we are." Louis said, "Yeah, that's why I brought all of that stuff with me. I figured it might come in handy, just in case we deal with something from the well."

As they headed out to the well, Norman looked at Louis and wondered if bringing his friend was the smart thing to do or not. I hope bringing Louis with me was not a bad idea or something.

They walked outside with a sudden breeze that brought a cold wave, and it chilled them as they were walking with the flashlight on, and they were approaching the field. As they entered, they felt the cold, wet weeds against their legs and they didn't expect the plants to be so clammy.

"How you doin', Louis?" Norman asked with concern, as he knew what could happen if they got caught, or if something happened with the well. He hoped that his thoughts were right and what happened to his pal was based on his imagination.

"Are you OK, Norman?" Louis asked as they were getting close, and they could see the well in the distance.

Norman stared at the well as they had approached it. He did not answer Louis's question, and Louis looked at quickly and then, he looked at the well with curious eyes, and he took out the hammer he grabbed from home.

Louis approached the well while Norman stood still nearby in the tall grass. Louis stood by the well while the brook behind him made a relaxing gurgling sound.

"Are we going to open this sucker or not, Norman?" he asked with a little agitation.

"Yes...we are doing this," Norman answered with great hesitation, and he slowly walks towards the well, and he placed his stuff down on the ground next to Louis's. Louis had put down his bag of goodies, and they each surrounded the well and pushed it to the right side.

"Here we go. On the count of three, we will push this, and hopefully, it will come off easily." Norman said with a firm voice. Louis noticed that his buddy was coming around and was becoming more like himself.

At the three counts, they pushed the cover with a strong shove and Louis saw down the well first before Norman. Louis could only see darkness, and he pointed the flashlight down the well, and he saw water, a few mice, and that was it. Everything was as expected.

"There's nothing, Norman." Louis felt foolish, and he kept thinking he would see something stick out or even be from another world.

Norman looked down while Louis had the flashlight pointed into the water, and he couldn't believe his eyes. What the hell is going on...?

Norman and Louis glanced down into the dark-murky water again, and then something was making bubbles. With their flashlights pointing directing on the bubbles, a stick-looking object started to come up through the water, breaking the surface and revealing itself above the murk.

"What the hell is that?!" Louis asked while his nerves shook a little as he looked directly at the stick that was slowly moving upwards.

Norman was speechless as he kept his flashlight pointed at the stuck object and then, it stopped.

The lights were directly on the stuck object, and the boys could almost see something following the stick. "HOLY SHIT!" Louis yelled, and then, a claw reached up and tried to grab Louis, but it got his jacket instead, and it was trying to pull him down into the well.

"NORMAN! NORMAN! HELP!" he screamed as Norman grabbed his friend. Louis was trying to get out of his jacket, and the claw had the front part of his jacket, just where the zipper was.

"GET OUT OF YOUR JACKET, LOUIS...SLIP OUT OF IT!"

"I'M TRYING...BUT IT'S GOT ME GOOD!" Norman kept pulling on Louis and finally the boy was free from the grips of the claw. Suddenly, the claw pulled hard, and Louis slipped out, and he jumped away from the well while pushing Norman to the side.

"WHAT THE HELL WAS THAT?!" Louis asked while taking deep breaths. He was shaking as Norman stared at the well and couldn't believe a claw came out of the well.

HOLY SHIT! A DAMN CLAW...FROM A WELL... He couldn't believe what he saw and what tried to grab Louis. The claw had been covered in green slime with stingers on the flat, which would be the palm of a hand. The claw's tips were like those of a crab but from something more insidious...

Louis and Norman sat on the cold, wet ground, just near the brook. They watched the well cover slowly close, seeing nothing moving beneath it. "What are we going to do, Norman?" Louis asked while trying to catch his breath.

"Shit! I have no idea! I might have to try and tell my parents. "Maybe even my Dad," Norman said while trying to remain calm, the back of his pants was cold and wet and some dirt on him after falling by the well.

The two boys sat far enough from the well with damp pants, their flashlights still beaming at the well and their faces sweaty. "I'm cold, Norman."

"Me too, Louis. We need to get back to my house and figure out what to do."

"I can't go back. I need to go home, Norman, and get to bed! If my parents discovered I'm not in bed...they'll kill me!" Norman looked at him briefly and nodded. They both sighed for a few minutes before growing a nerve and getting up and walking back.

"What happens if that thing gets out of the well and goes to your house... or mine?" Louis thought of it, and Norman assured him it wouldn't happen. But Louis had a terrible thought. What if... That thing comes out, pissed! Looking for Louis or me...shit! What would I Do? What would Louis do? The tall grass was like walking through the Scarborough Marsh in December and feeling all cold, wet and certain places...slimy.

"I'm sorry, Louis, for getting you involved and almost killed."

"It's not your fault, Norman, but what are you going to do?" Louis was concerned as he looked at his friend, who was not far from the well and whatever lived in it.

Norman looked at him briefly, and he felt bad and hoped that he would be okay for tonight, but he was a little scared based on Louis's assumptions. He would be sleeping lightly tonight himself.

The two boys got back to Norman's house, and Louis headed home. Norman didn't realize that Louis had his bike, which explained how quickly he got to his home. Norman went inside his house with grass stains on his pants. He knew his mother might discover the truth based on her observations of the kids' clothes. After going inside quietly, he walked into his sister Katie's room, but he knew if he woke her up, it would be a lot of trouble!

His footsteps were quiet, with the typical cracking of the floor that came with the house shifting a little due to the ground underneath settling. He closed his room's door to the hallway, and he took off his clothes, covered with splashes of well-water dirt.

He opened the door and went to the bathroom, closing the door. He turned the faucet on and washed his hands and face. He put his dirty clothes in the laundry basket, and he already had an excuse for his mother if she asked what had happened.

Mom, I forgot to put it all in the hamper after playing outside by the well. I'm sorry...

It was a good excuse, he guessed, but he was unsure and nervous whether it would work or not. After cleaning up, he went to his bedroom while tiptoeing his way to his room and hoping not to wake his sister or his parents. After putting on some shorts, he got into bed with his thoughts, dwelling on what would happen tonight with that thing in the well. Lying in bed with his head on his pillow, while the rest of his body was tucked nicely under the sheets.

He fell asleep with dreams – nightmares – of the creature in the well and seeing his furry friend become a bloody meal for it. His friend, Louis, had been grabbed by it and now, what the hell am I going to do with that thing?

The next day, morning came quickly, like a rogue wave knocking over a ship. He woke to the bed shaking and a voice telling him to, "Wake up and get ready for school." His eyes were heavy as if tiny dumbbells were sitting on the edges of his eyelids and preventing him from waking up.

"OK...I'm awake, Mom." His voice filled with a little irritation and his mother said it once more and, then, he got out of bed with his body still tired and half asleep. He had slept for five hours, and he looked to the palms of his hands and realized there were scratches and some scraps from last night's adventure.

Holy cow, my hands! He walked to the bathroom while hearing the voices of his sister and his parents talking and the aroma of breakfast filling the air. His taste buds salivated at the smell of bacon, eggs, and toast in the air...he was ready to eat! He walked into the kitchen where the yummy smell was the strongest, and he slowly sat down with his eyes fighting to stay open, and he looked over at his father, who was enjoying a cup of coffee with his plate almost empty. There were small bits of bacon and some yellow stains from the yolks left over.

Norman was given a plate of delicious delights. He glanced down at his place with his half-open eyes, and he slowly reached forward with his fork. He reached over and grabbed the full glass of orange juice that sat nicely, just on the top-right corner of his breakfast plate, and he lifted it and took a sip.

He pondered the situation and tried to wake up. He was tempted to ask his father for some of his coffee, but he already knew the answer. He slowly indulged himself in his meal, and he started with the eggs; which were a wet sunny-side up.

I might have to ask Dad for his coffee. I can't... I am so tired from last night. His sister watched him as if she waited for him to turn into a night creature. "Why are you staring at me?" he asked with irritation.

"I'm not staring at you, moron!"

"All right, that's enough! I'm not dealing with this stuff in the morning before work," their father said while finishing his coffee.

"You have thirty minutes to eat and shower, Norman," his mother said while she was working a little later.

"All right, Mom. I'm working on it." Norman's voice had a slight heaviness to it. Norman took his fork and dove into the eggs, and he ate again.

Norman ate and showered and was outside waiting for the bus to arrive. He kept looking towards the field where the well sat in place, with its hidden darkness dwelling within the rusted and cemented home.

He was concerned about Louis. I hope he got to rest last night, because I know I'm damn tired and could sleep until noon. I was even too tired to play with my video games and could only read a few of my comics.

Norman's bus arrived, and he got on while kids were yelling and playing games on their cell phones and texting each other, even texting the person next to them. Norman sat alone in the back, with his thoughts on the well and his need for sleep.

He sat back and looked down at his cell phone and was checking out pictures. A thought came to mind. What if I use a camera and record the activity? My cell could handle the water, but if not, my parents would kill me!

As the bus was moving and making stops, picking up kids, which added to the already loud bus, Norman developed a headache. His eyes were bouncing back and forth between looking out through the window and then glancing at his cell.

"Norman, you're quiet this morning. Are you OK?" a soft and low voice asked. He was surprised to hear it, considering the bus was so loud. He looked up and saw his friend, Shirley, and she was smiling and looking at him with her shining hazel eyes and light-brown hair. She was a little taller than Norman, but still the same age.

"I was just thinking about Denny, that's all," he said while glancing back and forth his phone and looking at her.

"I'm sorry, Norman. I remember when I lost Sadie, my cat. She was five, and she was sick and not getting better."

"How did she die?" Norman asked while trying to hold back a tear.

"She had gotten a cold and died shortly after. My parents have no clue how or why, but it took me months to get over it."

"It doesn't go away, though...right?" he asked while trying to fight tears from forming.

"It never does, but I know she's in a good place and someday...a long time from now, I will see her again," Shirley said while glancing at Norman. Sitting in the seat next to him, she liked him and knew he liked her.

Norman looked out the window as the bus was moving and stopping to pick up kids.

Shirley wanted to hold his hand but was afraid to. She feared it wasn't the right time, and she also didn't want to look like a fool in front of the other kids. Norman had the great urge to tell her, but he declined to do so.

At school, Norman sat in his desk chair, and he could never forget about the first time he got this seat. Damn gum was bulging out from where he worked on his assignments and sometimes it would hit his leg if he lifted it just right. I'm glad my teacher said something, and it was gone within days.

Norman hadn't seen Louis all day, and wondering what happened last night terrified him. He didn't want to come to school, not based on his being tired, but rather fearing whatever was in the well.

"Norman, are you alright?" his teacher, Mr. Hanley, asked. Norman looked at him and saw the concern on his face as he was holding his pencil in his right hand. Norman's eyes revealed something to him, but he didn't want to get embarrassed by the other kids.

"Is this something that needs to be discussed in person?"

Norman's eyes went down to the desk and nodded.

"OK. We'll talk after class," he said while he patted Norman's right shoulder, ensuring he was there for him. Class ended with a slightly high note, but Norman was somewhere else; he kept thinking about the well. "So, Norman. Tell me what's going on?" Mr. Hanley sat next to him with the car, making a scratching sound as he pulled the chair out, but it matched the other marks that had been by other students.

"I don't know what else to say, Mr. Hanley," Norman said softly.

"Is everything OK at home?" he asked.

"I lost my dog and something...something else is bothering me, too," Norman wanted to tell Mr. Hanley, but he was worried that he wouldn't believe him.

"Please tell me...what's going on?" Mr. Hanley said with a concerned look.

"My dog was killed by something in the well. I saw everything." Tears grew and trickled down his cheeks, and Mr. Hanley put his hand on his right shoulder, and he asked, "What killed your dog, Norman?"

Norman looked up at Mr. Hanley with his eyes flooded with tears and said, "A monster from the well did it." His words were sincere, and Mr. Hanley felt there was a deeper message there. He wanted to contact the guidance counselor, but Norman pleaded with him not to say anything.

"Did you see this monster that killed your dog, Norman?" Mr. Hanley asked while taking notes with his mind, looking for any clues that maybe there was more trouble at home, and Norman was using a 'monster' metaphor rather than describing his real problem.

"I saw part of it, and it had tentacles and ripped my dog in half, and then it went back into the well." He cried, and Mr. Hanley kept his hand on Norman's right shoulder, to remind him he was not alone, and it was all right to talk about it.

"Why do you think this 'monster' killed your dog?" Mr. Hanley asked.

"I don't know, but I'm afraid it's going to come out and get my folks and me."

"Do your parents know what happened?" Mr. Hanley asked.

"Yes."

"What was their answer?"

"I don't think they believe that a monster killed my dog, but they believe something did... they haven't said much."

"That's quite a story, Norman. Do you mind if I bring you home today? I want to check out this well for myself. Do you think your parents will be OK with that?" Mr. Hanley asked while getting up and seeing it was almost time to go. Norman sat in his chair while Mr. Hanley left the classroom to alert the bus driver he was driving him home instead. They got into Mr. Hanley's Ford Ranger. Norman sat quietly and grew concerned that maybe the monster from the well would get Mr. Hanley.

"Why so quiet?" Mr. Hanley asked as he was driving Norman home.

"Nothing except what's at home," he said as he looked out through the window and was worried about what might occur.

"Are you concerned about your well?"

"I am a little," Norman said sadly.

"I will go out with you and check it out if it's OK with your folks?"

"Mr. Hanley you don't have to go out...if you don't want to," Norman said with concern.

They were at Norman's house, and they walked into the house as Mr. Hanley introduced himself and told Norman's parents he was bringing him home, based on an earlier phone call.

A proper introduction was done as hands were shaking and Mr. Hanley said, "Norman has this concern about a 'well' in the field or something. That his dog was killed by a creature or something from the well," he said while Norman's father's eyes showed some concern as if he was worried Norman had said too much and his teacher wouldn't believe him.

"Norman has an interesting imagination, and I don't know what he told you, but it might be a little too far-fetched," his father said with his eyes switching back and forth between everyone.

"I know he has a vivid imagination, but have you checked out the history of this well?" Mr. Hanley asked while adjusting his glasses.

"I have, and I found nothing, but there were these weird etchings on the side. Maybe Spanish, or another language I'm not familiar with."

"May I go out and check?" Mr. Hanley asked, and the parents reluctantly agreed.

Ted walked with Jordan Hanley to the well and Norman trailed far behind as they were wading through the tall grass. Within minutes, they were at the well, and Norman was worried about his body wanting to stay behind, but he wanted to protect his father and Mr. Jordan Hanley.

Jordan saw the well, and he walked up to it and saw bloodstains on the outside rim, and he quickly looked at Norman and then back to the well, and he gently touched the bloodstain, which was dry due to the weather.

"Wow! Is there a way we can take the cover off?" he asked, his eyes filled with curiosity.

Ted was reluctant but agreed to Jordan's request. As they were both opening the lid, Jordan saw the writing that Ted mentioned and he adjusted his glasses, and he quickly took out his cell and took two photos of the writing. "Wow! This is very interesting," he said as the cover lay on the ground, and he was studying the writing while Norman was concerned about what was lurking in it. The writing read))))::: G)A((| \, but that was just some of it.

"This isn't Spanish, but something else," he said while he kept looking at it while looking down the well and seeing a reflection of himself.

"What do you mean?" Ted asked.

"This writing or language… it's almost English, but backward. I will I have to examine it when I get home and do some research."

He turned to Norman and asked, "So, Norman, what did you see come out of here?"

"As I said, I saw a monster kill Denny," he said, almost thinking that Mr. Hanley didn't believe him.

"I would suggest not looking down the well too long," Ted said with concern.

Jordan smiled and shrugged it off with a smile and asked, "Is this well connected to your house?"

"No, our personal well is an artisan and it's closer to the house."

Jordan looked down, and he gently reached out with his right hand, and he touched the water, and it was warm. "That's weird," he said.

"What's the matter?" Ted asked.

"The water is warm. It should be cold." Jordan was curious, and Norman grew worried that the monster would come out and get Mr. Hanley, but nothing.

Ted touched the water, and Norman told him, "No," but Ted still did so, and he couldn't believe how warm it was. "That's very warm," Ted said while the two were touching the water and the ripples went the opposite way.

"That's weird," Jordan said with his eyes revealing some disbelief.

"What's the matter?" Ted asked.

"The ripples are going the opposite direction when we touch it, where it should be coming from hands, but more like towards it..." Suddenly, Mr. Hanley was pulled into the water with a quick SPLASH! Ted grabbed him, and he was trying to pull him up. "SOMETHING'S GOT ME!" he screamed, and Ted told Norman to run!

Ted was trying to pull Jordan up, but something was dragging the man downwards into the darkness.

"HANG ON!" Ted was pulling Jordan, then...The man's arms ripped off, and blood gushed out like a popped blood vessel, and Jordan screamed and then...he was pulled under! Ted fell backward and screamed. Blood was on his face and his upper torso, and he yelled bloody murder. He was shaking, and he stared at the well. He could hear the scream muffled in the warm, bloodied water and couldn't believe what happened! Norman fell to the ground with his hands shaking, and he looked at his father, and his father shook while covered with water and blood.

Jordan's arms flapped a little as the nerve endings were still alive and Norman screamed, and Ted looked at the water, ignoring the flapping limbs, and he slowly stood up, and he walked up to the well while trying to hear from Jordan, but nothing.

"Dad? DAD?" Norman called to his father, who stood still and then, he slowly backed away, and he looked at the well, and he slowly looked at Norman and walked towards the house.

"Dad? Dad?! Are you OK, Dad?" Norman asked while following him and his father didn't respond, but he was quiet, and he was walking towards the house. Ted made it to the house, and he walked towards the bathroom, and he quickly turned the faucet on and washed his face and looking at himself in the mirror.

His wife came in and asked what happened. "Ted? Ted, what happened?"

After washing his face, he slowly looked at his wife and stuttered, "We have a monster in the well." His wife asked again, and he said once more, "We have a monster in the well."

She saw the blood and her eyes widened, and she looked at Norman, who was standing behind her and deep down inside, she believed him. After cleansing his face, Ted went into the bedroom, and she asked about

Jordan, and Ted told her everything. "What kind of monster is it?" she asked, trying to believe what he told her.

Ted looked down at his knees, and they were shaking, revealing his fear and the truth behind his belief on what happened to his son's teacher.

"Dad? Dad? Dad, what are we going to do?" Norman asked while walking into the bedroom and looking at his father.

Ted slowly looked down at Norman and said, "We're gonna kill the fucker!" A smirk slowly grew across Norman's face, and he rushed

***

In the driveway, Norman's mother stood with their daughter. "Where are you going to go?" Ted asked while Norman stood beside him.

"Do you realize what you're saying?" she asked while getting out of the car and confronting him, trying to make him understand.

"I know it sounds crazy, but honey, you have to see what thing did!"

"It does sound crazy to me. A monster is living in the old well, killing people." Ted understood what she was saying, but she hadn't seen the horror in action yet. He wanted to show her, but he was worried about the creature coming out and getting them all.

He didn't know if the thing could survive without the well or water, either. But he knew he had to do something.

"OK. For one brief moment, I believe you. Do you know how this thing got there?" Her question brought up a good point, and Ted sincerely thought about what she asked and felt that doing a little research would help.

Ted got online, and he checked the history of the address, and nothing came up, but the propaganda of good water gone bad in Minnesota, and Ted kept typing and still got nothing. He knew he would have to go to the town hall and check records of previous owners.

"Honey, anything?" Wilma asked while attending to make dinner, and the kids were sitting at the dining table. Norman was the only one who was not hungry, but Wilma wanted to keep everyone and their thoughts on other things.

She considered calling 9-1-1, but the problem was they could be accused of murder or suddenly responsible for a missing person case. She suppressed those dark thoughts and focused on dinner.

"I need to go to the town hall tomorrow morning and find out who the previous owners were," Ted said while going to the bathroom and taking a shower. As the hot water was raining down upon him, he could feel the well's residue running down his body and into the drain. He wasn't very dirty physically, but he felt filthy after seeing the things he saw. I didn't think things like that existed. I thought they were fairy tales or something. Norman tried telling me, but I didn't listen. Stupid me got a teacher killed. But, what the hell is in that well?

"Norman, did you wash up before sitting down?" His mother asked, and the boy nodded. His face was pale, and he couldn't believe his mother was preparing dinner after seeing his teacher being ripped apart by a creature in the well.

Meanwhile, Ted got out of the shower and grabbed a towel hanging on the rack. He thought about the teacher and the image of Jordan screaming and being dragged down into the well.

Norman looked at his food, which was baked ham with boiled white rice and sliced carrots. Katie stared at him as if his ears were growing larger than his face or crabs were coming out of his mouth.

Norman gently picked up his fork, and he slowly forked his carrots into his mouth while Ted was contemplating calling the police and reporting on what happened, but then decided not to do so.

Guilt filled Ted's eyes, and he just hoped that the teacher had no family. Norman was eating a little as he kept looking at his father, concerned about him. He knew that his father was experiencing the pain that Norman felt the first time after losing his dog. I hope you're OK, Dad...

Ted was sitting down with tears in his eyes as he wasn't sure what to do. Either way, he didn't want Norman involved.

Norman kept looking at him and knew he had seen something Norman had been trying to tell him, but his father didn't believe him until now. He wasn't sure about his mother, but she was doing her best, keeping everyone calm, but she knew something was wrong. "What can we do?" she asked while looking at Ted and Norman, and they both wore the same look. Ted slowly peered up at her and said, "We need to kill it." She looked at him, shocked, and Norman said, "I agree, Dad."

The dinner in front of Norman and Ted was getting warm, and they both were not hungry, especially after what happened to Norman's teacher. She looked at the both of them and asked, "OK. I'm trying to be calm, but how?" she asked.

Ted's online research brought up nothing, and Norman thought maybe his friends would know. Norman knew Louis would be scared to come back over, but maybe Shirley could help?

***

The next day, it was a Saturday, and Norman called Shirley. She came over when her mother could drive her over. She went into Norman's bedroom, where he was sitting on the bed with his knees up to his chest as if he was rolled up. She walked over to him and sat next to him on the bed, wrapping her left arm around and kissing him on the cheek.

"What was that for?" he said, shocked.

She smiled and said, "I've wanted to do that for a quite some time now." Norman blushed, but the new feeling brought comfort, and when she told him how she felt, he was genuinely surprised. He had some idea, but not to this magnanimity.

"So, why did you want me to come over – well, besides me kissing you..." she chuckled.

"I want you to believe me about something, and please don't laugh when I tell you."

"OK. I won't."

"You promise?"

"Yes."

Norman told Shirley what had been going on, and he told her that Louis was attacked and that he refused to come back over. After fifteen minutes of telling her, she stood up with a surprised look and slowly turned around, and she looked down at Norman, who was sitting in a normal position and... "That's why you've been a little different at school, and it wasn't about me, it was about this...this well?" He looked up at her and nodded. "I gotta see this thing so that we know what we're dealing with."

Her curiosity worried Norman, but she wanted to record the entire incident, and he stood up, thinking she was crazy, but she could be right! "OK, so, will a cell phone work at night?" he asked.

"If your cell has a night vision lens, we can use it. If not, we would have to shine a light on it when it comes out," she said, thinking and suggesting ideas. "Who's got a good camera, though?" he asked.

"Louis has an awesome camera. Remember, his father does video work for companies."

"That might be a bad idea, roping in Louis." A voice was heard from the other room, and then, in came Norman's father.

"I could overhear your conversation. You want to record this...thing?" he asked.

"Oh, hi, sir. Yes. With the four of us, we might be able to get something."

"I already told you, Louis will not come back here," he said while watching the two argue over Louis and the fancy camera that his father owned.

"Let me talk to him, Norman?" Shirley asked, and Ted said, "Shirley, you have no idea what you're dealing with. I cannot allow you to be part of this." He then yelled at Norman about telling his friends, but she calmed the angry man down.

"We need to find out what we're dealing with, sir. Louis will help, I'm sure." Her words were optimistic, and Ted wasn't sure he could protect them both, but he knew something had to be done about the thing in the well!

Louis agreed to help, but with great resistance. Norman, Shirley, and Louis were heading out to the well while Ted's parents were preparing a little surprise of their own as they wanted to trap whatever was going on.

"Holy shit! I cannot believe you got me to go with you," Louis said while carrying a baseball bat and Norman and Shirley were carrying a bag full of possible items that would be helpful, including a swimmer's goggles and snorkel tube for breathing.

"Don't worry about it," Norman said, and even though his parents were helping, the deal was that they would wait for his parents to show up and then they would proceed with the mission, but Norman wanted to go into the well by himself, not endangering anyone he cared about.

"I can't believe you're going down by yourself, Norman," Shirley said with concern as they arrived at the well and Louis wanted to hang back. Norman promised $30 to Louis and Shirley if they helped him.

"I want to know what it is," Norman said while putting down the bag of supplies. Shirley had a flashlight, and she had a lead pipe she got from her father's garage. Norman reached into the bag and grabbed the swimmer's goggles and the tube. He knew that he might have to go underwater and that the breathing snorkel would be useless, leaving him to drown.

He looked over and saw his parents outside, and while his mother had kept insisting on calling the police, his father told her they wouldn't believe them and could make things worse.

Norman, Shirley, and Louis were at the well, and Norman put on his swimming goggles, and he got his snorkel ready. "Are you sure you want to do this?" Shirley asked with great worry in her voice, and Louis looked at him and said, "Well, it was nice knowing you, pal." Shirley bopped him firmly on the arm, and he responded with an, "Ow!"

All three pushed the cover off the well, which at first was hard as Louis was hesitant and terrified, but then, they finally did it, and they flashed their lights down into the dark water. There was a rank odor, a musty smell of an ancient evil.

"What the hell is that?" Louis asked while holding his nose, and Shirley agreed. Norman could smell it a little but ignored it, and he gripped his baseball bat and a small jackknife.

"Do you want something bigger?" Shirley asked while showing him what she brought from home – a machete. "Holy shit! This should do it!" He thanked her. She smiled and then, she reached into the bag and grabbed the rope.

Louis and Shirley tied one end of the rope to the wooden post while Norman tied the other one around his waist. He slowly climbed onto the edge of the well and Louis kept his distance while Shirley remained by his side.

Norman slowly climbed into the well, and within two and a half feet, he would be touching water. Norman trembled as he slowly got into the water, not knowing if the creature would suddenly appear and swallow him like a scene from Jaws.

He climbed down into the well while holding the machete in one hand and gripping a bag of a few things he grabbed from his parent's garage in the other, and his feet touched the cold water, and he cried out, "Shit! That's cold!"

"Don't say anything! Remain quiet," Shirley said, while her eyes were scanning the well and flashing the light into the dark. She could not see the bottom. Norman was now submerged in the cold water except for his head, and he briefly said, "Here I go. Kill anything that isn't me!"

Shirley nodded, and Louis also agreed, holding the baseball bat that Norman had brought. As Louis and Shirley held onto the rope and Norman lowered himself into the well, he suddenly thought of two movies. They were The Cave and The Descent. As he was underwater and he had his flashlight on, and he grew more and more worried that the creature would come and get him.

As he lowered himself deeper with his mask, he noticed that it was made to hold air, but only for a few minutes at a time. The snorkel had a filter on it, where it kept water from coming in, but Norman only expected to be down in the well for no longer than ten minutes, depending on if he could tell where the creature was coming from.

As he slowly lowered himself, even more, he could feel the mask growing tighter on his face, and he knew his air would run out until he held his breath. Suddenly, there was a force pulling on him. It was dragging him, and he tried to fight it, and then, he was swept forcefully down a passage, ending up in an air pocket.

He took full advantage of it, and he trembled heavily with fear, as he couldn't believe where he was. His body had been pulled by some current, and as he let go, he ended up in the air pocket that was just under the edges of the well.

He wondered how this was possible. This was only an old well, but it was something more, but what? His thoughts stopped as suddenly he heard splashing within the cement walls and the hideous smell loomed heavily, but he ignored it and focused on the splashing he heard. Suddenly, something grabbed him, and it was his father. "Dad, what are you doing here?"

"Norman, you're my son, and you shouldn't be down here. This was my job, not yours."

"How is this possible?" Norman asked while looking around, and the only lights were those from him and his and father. "I'm not sure, but I am wondering if this well is somehow connected to a canal that had been blocked when it was first built," his father said while looking around and seeing their space was limited at least six feet.

"Dad, we must kill the thing, or it might hurt someone else."

"Norman, I know, but we have no idea what we're dealing with." Norman saw that his father had no rope connected to him.

My dad dove into the well...that's so damn cool! "Alright, here's the plan. We must keep that rope tied around your waist at all times. We cannot use it for anything else other than safety," he said, and Norman nodded in agreement.

"OK, there's an opening, and I can feel the pull. There must be a current of some sort."

"Me too."

Norman and his father tried to find something to hang onto the walls, and they found small crevices they could climb.

"At the count of three, we're going to dive and follow that current, okay?" his father said, and Norman was worried because his father didn't have a snorkel, though he had eye goggles, his noise was still exposed. "One...two...THREE!"

They descended into the deep water, and Norman followed his father. Sure enough, there was a current and carried them a little, and then, they hit another air pocket and then ascended.

"Are you OK?" His father asked while looking around and checking Norman's goggles.

"I'm OK. How are you, Dad?"

"I'm fine. I'm just dumbfounded by the hell we're in, that's all," his father said while looking around; he couldn't believe this was part of the well. Norman was dumbfounded too but was more concerned about the creature.

"Where's the monster?" Norman asked while looking around, and he was frightened.

"I'm hoping that damn thing swam out, but we must be on guard, even though we can't see anything unless I watch the road ahead and you watch our back, agreed?" He smiled, and Norman smiled back.

"I love you, Norman. We're going to survive this," Ted said while seeing the great concern on his son's face. He knew it wasn't wise for him to keep Norman down here, but he could see Norman wanted to avenge his beloved dog.

"Here we go, another swim." They adjusted their goggles and said, "One...Two...Three!"

They descended again, and suddenly, a sudden rush took them, and they got separated.

"NORMAN?!" "DAD?!" They both screamed as they were separated. There were two small tunnels, and they both went separately. Norman was being rushed, and then, he found an air pocket, and he screamed! He was crying for his father. "DAD?" DAD?" There was no answer, and he yelled out again, "DAD?" DAD." There was no response. His voice trembled with deep fear.

Norman looked around and saw that the water was rushing in two directions like before. A single thought implanted itself in his mind, and it was about the creature. Where was it hiding its hideous face?

Norman gripped the corners of the walls, and he slowly approached the intersection. Even though the water pressure was strong, it was not enough for him to lose balance. He wasn't able to touch the floor, so he had to swim a little.

He looked down into the two corridors, and he had to choose where his father might be, but which one was it? He thought while grinding his teeth a little. He went right, but then as he was doing so, he could hear his father's voice in the left corridor, and he fought the current while holding on and made his way into the left tunnel. The current was strong, and as he was being carried, he looked at the ceiling of the tunnels and could see vines covered with green moss and then, there was a quick dip and he went over.

The dip was a like waterfall, but not as high and deep. He screamed, and his feet hit the water first, and he swam to the surface, and he immediately yelled for his father, to no response. He looked around, and he could see that he was in a new chamber.

The chamber looked to be part of a bigger room. The vines engulfed the ceiling with green moss, and there were strands of white hair that covered it as well. Norman looked around as he couldn't believe what he was seeing. He hoped he could find his father and try to kill the creature; if not, he would hope to escape and try another day.

Ted glanced at his surroundings and saw that he was stuck in vines. The green moss slightly covered his legs and he reached into his front pocket and pulled out a jackknife and was able to pull out the blade and cut the vines, but it wasn't strong enough.

He pulled out the saw blade, and it worked. Within five minutes, he was free, and his focus was finding Norman and getting out. Killing the creature would have to wait and finding a way out with Norman was now his top priority.

He swam along with the merciless current, and as the tunnel of ahead became bigger and bigger, he looked around and saw bones and dead leaves. He couldn't believe what he was seeing and immediately called out for Norman. He did so twice but heard nothing.

He hoped that Norman was okay. If that son of a bitch did something to my boy, I would kill that fucker! He kept swimming slowly as the bones on the sides were becoming more and more evident and then he saw a dense clearing, but he wasn't sure where it led to. He approached with caution while swimming and not able to feel the bottom of this ugly hellhole.

Norman was swimming, but he kept to the side while hanging onto the dead and withered vines, knowing that one of them could easily break. He kept thinking about his finding his father and getting out. He did wonder about one thing, and that was where this damn creature was lurking that came down here to kill.

"Dad? Dad?" He kept yelling for his father but received nothing in return — only echoes of his voice in the dark tunnels of the well. The water got warmer and murkier, as he wasn't able to see anything.

His backpack was tied tightly, and everything he needed was inside the pack. The tunnels were like mazes. Every time he came to a crossroads, he either had to make a choice, or at times he was forced depending on the current.

"Dad? Dad?" He hoped his father was okay. Ted held onto a vine and the body count continued as he saw skeletons along the walls, and some were of them were so bunched up they formed islands in the water like a morbid coral reef.

As he stopped while hanging on, he was catching his breath. The water was still cold, but it slowly grew warmer. He was a little satisfied that the water was getting warmer because of his fear of hypothermia. He was a very concerned that the creature had gotten Norman and it was still around, lurking in the shadows watching Ted like a snake, allowing Ted to flee and struggle to torture him.

Ted hoped that the creature was nowhere in sight, but he continued to pray internally.

He felt the current slowing down, which meant he was getting close to something, but he did not understand what. I can't wait until Norman, and I are outta here. I dunno if he's okay or not, but please God...protect my son. Ted suddenly felt something round and very wet and realized that it was an eyeball. He freaked out and sighed as he went back to the wall of vines and skeletons as he watched the corpse go with the current and he hoped it wasn't Norman.

One of the nerve endings got hung up on a limb, and he wanted to push it off, but he wasn't sure what would happen. From movies, he knew that there was usually a big surprise waiting for you on the other end. Please break off and flow with the current.

He kept moving, and his feet still weren't able to touch the bottom. He kept looking back, hoping the eyeball was still latched on the limb. The current brought him to an opening, and suddenly, he went over, and he screamed, and he ended up over in a small waterfall.

He landed abruptly, and he got up to the surface and swallowed water, immediately vomiting the filthy water. He did this a couple of times, and he watched the vomit go down with the current. The waterfall was not big, but big enough to carry his whole body and he turned up and looked at the height, and it was a solid one-hundred-foot drop. He looked around and wanted to see what his surroundings were like, and it had gotten worse.

Ted heard only his echoes of his voice calling for Norman and the sounds of the current of water moving quietly. He heard a smooth sound that could relax anyone, but the surroundings were rife with skeletons, and he suddenly saw chunks of flesh and Ted realized one thing...he was closer to the creature's lair now.

"Dad? Dad?" Norman yelled out again, but nothing. He stopped while the current firmly pressed against his body and was moving down the tunnels and then suddenly, he went over the large waterfall, and he landed feet-first.

After reaching the surface, he was lucky not to swallow any of the toxic water, and he looked around and saw there were more vines and some skeletons. He screamed as he also saw his teacher's torso tangled up, and Norman screamed until he heard yelling. He stopped and then, he listened again, and it was his father.

He swam towards the yelling and the voice of his father and then...he was in It's a lair. "HOLY SHIT!" Norman was now engulfed in an ooze mixed with the bad water, and the creature hung up on the wall, and it slithered its way down the vines.

The creature had a snake's head, but the rest of the body was almost like an octopus. The tentacles were hairy and had suction cups on the ends, but then they revealed what was inside, and there were long sharp claws, that looked like razors.

Norman couldn't scream, silent and shocked at what he was seeing. He heard crunching sounds coming from its hideous mouth. It had been eating another animal; a local cat.

Norman watched in awe and crouched cautiously, and then the creature spoke, emulating his father's voice. Norman asked what it wanted, and the creature looked at Norman, its greenish eyes blinking as it continued feeding.

A hand grabbed his shoulder from behind, and Norman screamed, and it was his true father.

"Norman, are you OK?" Ted was hugging his son, and Norman hugged him back.

"I'm...I'm alright, Dad."

"How did you find me, Norman?" his father asked.

"I heard you calling for me, Dad." Ted then realized the boy wasn't him, but it was...the creature.

"It was you?" Norman shouted, and the creature looked at Norman and nodded.

Its skin was pale green and slimy. A slight ooze came from its nose, and the creature unfolded its tongue, and it licked its nose. Which was two holes in its skull, like a snake, and Norman and his father grew sick at the sight?

"What do you want with us?" Ted yelled as he and Norman watched it devour its meal, and then it grew closer to them, and they slowly backed off, but it didn't get into the water. It moved around on the vines and using its tentacles like twigs to move around.

"What the fuck are you?" Ted asked, holding his son close, and he thought about how he would grab the things they needed from the backpacks and try to destroy the creature, sending it back to the hell it came from.

After finishing up its meal, the creature slowly slithered over to them, moving on the surface, but this was no snake. Ted did not understand what it was, but he knew what it wanted.

The creature gently touched the water, and the scales on its body were vibrating. Ted pulled Norman back while Norman was in disbelief at what he was seeing. He felt his father's gentle pull, and he went with it.

"Norman, let's go!" Ted said while looking behind and seeing there was an opening.

With their feet touching the water's depths, which felt like a muddy bottom, suddenly, the creature lunged at them. Norman punched the creature in its hideous face, and the creature screamed, and then, Ted said loudly, "Norman, let's go!"

They ran, not realizing they were running in water, which was waist-high for Ted, and they were moving as fast as they could while seeing the mini waves dispersing behind them, feeling the cold breath of the creature when Ted saw an opening. "Over there, Norman!" It was a tunnel, and with Norman by his father's side, they took a turn and noticed the water getting a little deeper, and Ted went forward. "Dad, the creature is behind us!" Ted could feel Norman trembling.

Ted stopped and grabbed Norman's backpack, and he took out a .44 pistol, and he aimed in the direction of the creature, and he stood still while holding the firearm tightly in his grasp.

Ted peered at the mini waves and knew the creature was coming while Norman held the backpack by the strap and they were looking around. BOOM! The creature shoved Norman to the wall, and Ted fired the gun, and one bullet nicked its head, and there was a slight squeal, and Ted ran over to Norman and, "Norman, are you OK?" Norman got up from the water, and Ted asked again, and Norman nodded.

"Let's go!" Ted grabbed Norman, and Norman found the backpack, and his grip was slightly loose, and he had the wind knocked out of him, but he was OK. "Dad, over there!"

Norman saw another tunnel, and there were more skeletons and islands. They were running, and they saw more skeletons and pieces of rotting flesh. "Norman, don't look!"

Ted led the way while making sure Norman was near, and as they entered the tunnel, the water had been receding. The water level was almost knee-high, and they ran a little faster, and they saw more bodies, and the smell was tedious and grotesque. That weird nauseating feeling grew in Norman's throat, but he covered his mouth, and he kept focused on what lay ahead.

"There's has to be a way out!" Ted looked around, and Norman followed suit. Suddenly, the mini waves were back, which meant that the creature was coming. "Norman...RUN!" Norman ran while Ted walked backward while looking behind him, making Norman was doing ok, and then, it was coming, and coming fast!

Ted took a few shots as he stared at the creature and two of the four shots fired, one bullet hit and penetrated the creature's left eye, and the other one pierced the creature's main tentacles. It screeched, and Ted fired again, but he was out of bullets. He kept the pistol and ran while Norman stopped and waited for him.

The creature slithered through the murky water, and yellow blood was oozing from its wounds. Ted and Norman kept running and then, they fell over a waterfall, and they screamed and landed in eight feet of dark water. Ted and Norman lost touch, and they both made it to the surface, and Ted ran over to Norman, who was stunned, but okay.

"Norman, are you all right?" He asked with great concern.

"Dad, I'm fine. Are we gonna get outta here?" Norman swam with his father, and the question planted a concern within Ted, but he kept remained strong. As they were swimming side by side, the backpack was heavy and weighing Norman down, but Ted helped him to swim, and then, they saw a current ahead of them. "Norman, there's another current. Let's take it!" Ted said loudly, and he held Norman's hand.

The current was great in force, and suddenly they feel could it rising. Ted hoped it led to their well, but it seemed like a different route. With all of the tunnels down there, anything was possible. Ted thoughts came to a halt while suddenly they were shot up and the force from behind was great, pushing them upwards.

Within a minute, Norman spotted something ahead, and he said, "Dad, we're close to the well." Ted looked ahead, and he saw a red marker. Norman told him he previously recorded it to keep track of their whereabouts, and Ted smiled.

The great force stopped abruptly, and they were swimming to the marked spot. Ted looked to his left side and saw other tunnels. "We must think it went down those other tunnels, but how did he do this?"

Ted was looking at his son, but he was also looking around while they held onto some vines on the walls. "When you went down that tunnel, I was able to mark it. I did it while I was being carried, and it's something you always taught me about directions." They embraced, and Ted told Norman he was proud of him and his survival skills.

They were holding onto the vines and then, they saw a small light from the surface. Ted said, "This might be the well, but where is that light coming from?" Norman checked his watch, and it showed 7 A.M. "Holy shit! We've been down here all that Time?" Ted was in disbelief, and Ted looked at Norman and told him, "Norman, we have to destroy the well." His words uttered with a mix of hope and concern.

By blowing up the well, they hoped it would destroy the creature, or, on the downside, it could free it. They wanted to destroy it. They grew closer to the opening, and they both looked up, and the light grew bigger, and they laughed. Norman said, "Dad, I found the rope."

"Norman, climb the rope." His father held it for him and started quickly looking back.

"Dad, what about you?" Norman asked with concern.

"I'll be right behind you, Norman. Now...GO!" His father yelled as he saw the water was making ripples at the creature coming. Norman climbed while his father held the backpack and he waited for Norman to climb the rope. Norman was yelling at his family and friends to pull him up.

At first, there was no response, then he heard his mother, and suddenly, the rope was pulled. Norman climbed halfway while he was slowly being pulled up and Ted wanted to start climbing, but suddenly, the creature ensnared Ted with its tentacles and Ted went flying into the wall.

Norman looked down and yelled for his father. The creature looked up at Norman, and the creature's pupils were fiery red, and Norman screamed. The creature climbed with its tentacles, grabbing the rope, and a yellow ooze was left behind everywhere it touched.

Ted stood up while the toxic water was up to his neck and he grabbed the creature's last tentacle, and it snarled, and then, he pulled it down, and it fell into the water. Ted started to climb the rope, and he quickly looked up and saw that Norman had made it out.

The rope was slippery with a yellow slime, and Ted ignored it, and he climbed. A couple of times, he almost lost his grip, based on the rope being slippery. He had the backpack tangled loosely off his back, but it was still after this.

"I'M COMIN' UP!" he yelled, but no response. The creature slowly rose like a dark ship ascending from the depths of hell, and it revealed its demonic pupils. Ted tried to climb faster, but he was slipping a little.

The rope got pulled from above, and Ted yelled again. "IT'S ME! PULL ME UP!" The pull was slow but steady. Ted used his feet to grip the rope, but the ooze or slime made it difficult. Ted was halfway there, and he felt the creature gripping the rope, trying to pull them down, and Ted knew he had to climb faster.

The brightness from the outside quickly blinded the creature, and it screeched. As Ted was climbing, he could feel the creature behind, suddenly, the rope broke just below Ted, and the creature fell and splashed into the bad water. "HOLY SHIT! THAT WAS CLOSE!" As he was climbing the rest of the rope, the creature leaped up, and it was clambering on the side of the wall like a spider. Ted's eyes widened as he couldn't believe what he was seeing, watching as the creature was able to get to the top. Ted thought of this new horrific development and then, a hand reached out, and it was his wife.

He grabbed her hand and felt the warmness of her skin and the rest of them helped her pull him up, and he yelled, "THE SMALL CAN OF GASOLINE IN THE BACKPACK, TAKE IT OUT AND POUR IT INTO THE WELL!"

"ARE YOU SURE?!" she asked while holding the backpack, but instead she took it out and pulled the cap off, and she started to pour the gasoline into the well and around the edges.

"IS THIS GONNA WORK?" she yelled, and she threw the rest of the red plastic can into the well, and Ted said, "HELL YES!" Norman took out the matches, and he tried to light them, but nothing happened, and Ted did the same.

"HOLY SHIT! WE NEED A LIGHTER!" Ted screamed, and then, Anna looked in her jacket pocket and found matches. "I was going to make coffee this morning, and I'm glad I didn't put this away." Ted kissed her and then, he tried to light a match by scratching it, but nothing.

Suddenly, the matches fell on the ground; he hoped the matches didn't get soaked because of the damp grass from overnight, and Norman grabbed a match. Suddenly, one of the tentacles grabbed Norman's left arm, and he screamed. His mother and father tried to free him, but Norman grabbed a jackknife he had in his pocket, and he cut into the tentacle, and he heard screeching. "NORMAN...LIGHT IT UP!" His father screamed, and Norman stabbed the creature in the tentacle, and suddenly, the creature let go, and it was screaming and screeching, and everyone had to cover their ears.

BOOOOM!!! Inside the well, the explosion blew the top off with pieces of cement landing in different parts of the field, and the fire was great and furious. The top of the well was heavily damaged, and the fire roared, and the family and Norman's friends slowly got up, and they looked over to the well and were stunned by what they saw.

Ted slowly got up while looking at the well and helping Norman and Katie. She pointed at the well, and they saw burnt tentacles and pieces of green and yellow flesh. Some pieces were dangled on the rigged edges of the well interior and the remains of the top of the well.

The creature had been destroyed, and Ted and Norman walked close up to the well while Ted kept his right arm in front, trying to keep him at a safe distance. The sunlight beamed warmly on their necks while Ted looked down the well and saw that the whole interior of the well was charred.

Suddenly, the creature appeared, and its head made it to the top while everyone screamed. The head of the creature suddenly came to a rest and the remainder of its body slowly detached and landed hard in the murky water, and the creature's empty and dark eyes stared out at the horrified family.

Ted and Norman as they stood still and Ted held Norman tightly, and suddenly, the head fell over onto the dirt, and a green ooze slid out of its mouth, and the eyes moved quickly. Everyone screamed again and then...the creature was dead.

You can find out more about the author and his work on his website.

Please visit www.horrorwriterduanecoffill.com.

The Well

Duane E. Coffill

CPSIA information can be obtained
at www.ICGtesting.com
Printed in the USA
LVHW041358140123
736914LV00008B/775